Fancy NANCY

Girl on the Go
A Doodle and Draw Book

Based on *Fancy Nancy* written by Jane O'Connor
Cover illustration by Robin Preiss Glasser
Interior illustrations by Aleksey and Olga Ivanov

HARPER FESTIVAL
An Imprint of HarperCollins Publishers

HarperFestival is an imprint of HarperCollins Publishers.

Fancy Nancy: Girl on the Go: A Doodle and Draw Book
Text copyright © 2012 by Jane O'Connor
Illustrations copyright © 2012 by Robin Preiss Glasser
All rights reserved. Manufactured in China.
No part of this book may be used or reproduced in any manner whatsoever without written permission except in the case of brief quotations embodied in critical articles and reviews.
For information address HarperCollins Children's Books, a division of HarperCollins Publishers, 10 East 53rd Street, New York, NY 10022.
www.harpercollinschildrens.com

ISBN 978-0-06-188282-1

Design by Sean Boggs
12 13 14 15 16   SCP   10 9 8 7 6 5 4 3 2 1
❖
First Edition

Backyard Explorer

Nancy has an adventurous spirit.
(That's a fancy way of saying she loves to go exploring.)
One of her favorite places to explore is her own backyard.
Draw a perfect explorer's outfit for her.

Nancy writes a note to Bree and puts it in their special mail basket. Decorate the note.

Help Nancy and Bree get ready by circling all the things you think they will need.

Make Nancy's chapeaus fancy.
(That's French for hats and you say it like this: shah-POS.)

Here is Nancy and Bree's clubhouse. Help them decorate it.

Today JoJo spots a very rare butterfly.
(Rare is fancy for unusual and special.)
Decorate the butterfly's wings.

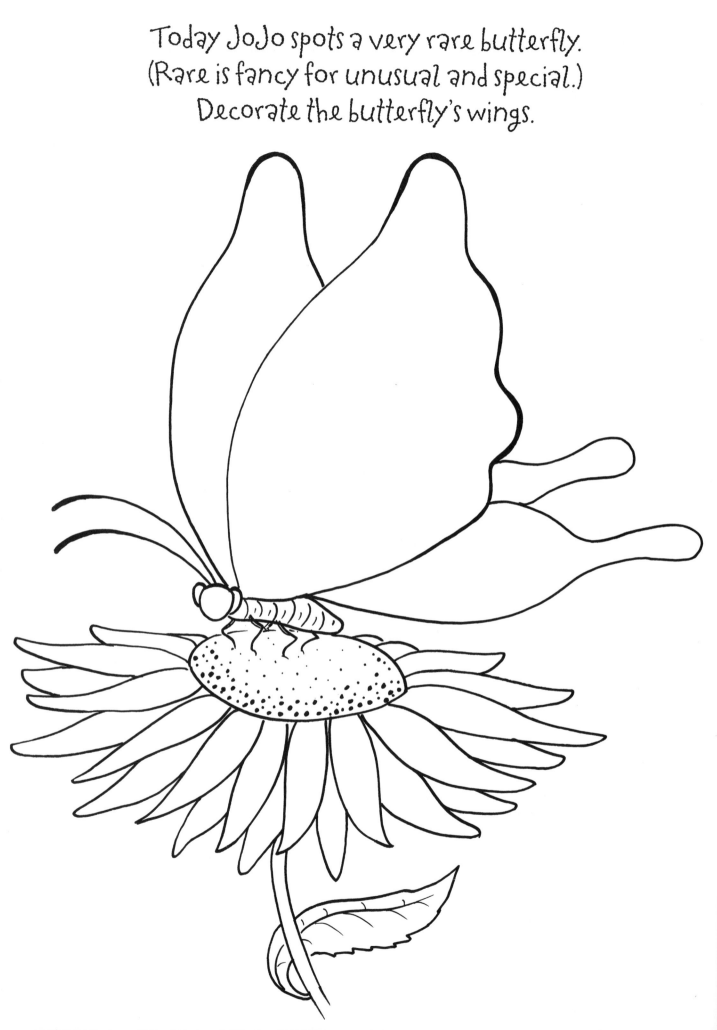

JoJo wears perfume to attract more butterflies.
Connect the dots to draw a perfume bottle.

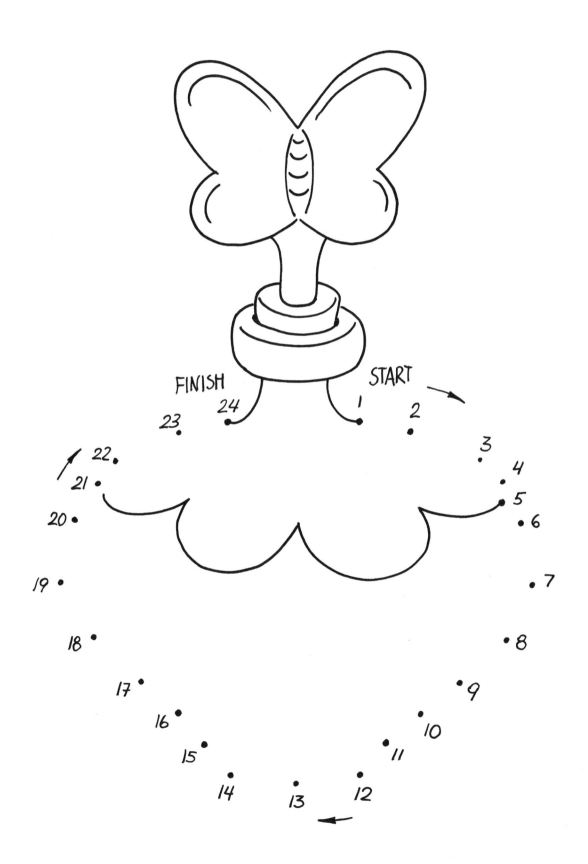

Which two butterflies are the same? Circle them.

Look! Bree has spotted a beautiful bird up in a tree.
Help Nancy get through the maze so she can see the bird too.

FINISH

START

Oh no! These baby robins need a nest.
Draw one with sticks and leaves—and, of course, you may
also add ribbons and a little umbrella for when it's sunny!

Nancy has a scrapbook with all the leaves she has collected.
Draw the other half of each leaf.

Maple Leaf

Oak Leaf

Oh no! It's raining. Draw each girl a posh umbrella.

The Neighborhood

Today Nancy is setting off on an excursion
(that's fancy for trip), but her bicycle is too plain.
Help her make it fancy!

Bree and JoJo are bike riding too! Connect the dots to draw JoJo's tricycle.

Nancy desires (that's fancy for wants) a yummy treat at the ice-cream shop. Draw Nancy's ultimate ice-cream cone. (And don't forget the cherry on top!)

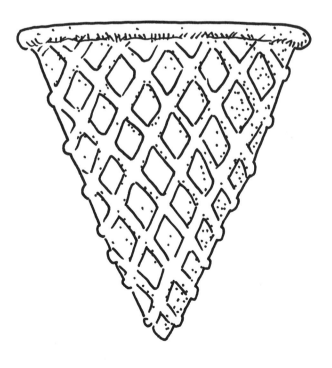

There are so many cool shops and boutiques downtown.
(A boutique is a fancy word for a fancy store.)
Draw what is in the store windows.
Make up a name for each store and write the name
on the sign.

The girls try on many pairs of shoes.
Which ones should they wear?
Match each pair.

Bree likes the scarf Nancy has on.
Find and circle one exactly like it for Bree.

Ooh la la! Nancy is getting a manicure—how glamorous!
Color in her nails with your favorite colors.
Then draw some fancy rings on her fingers.

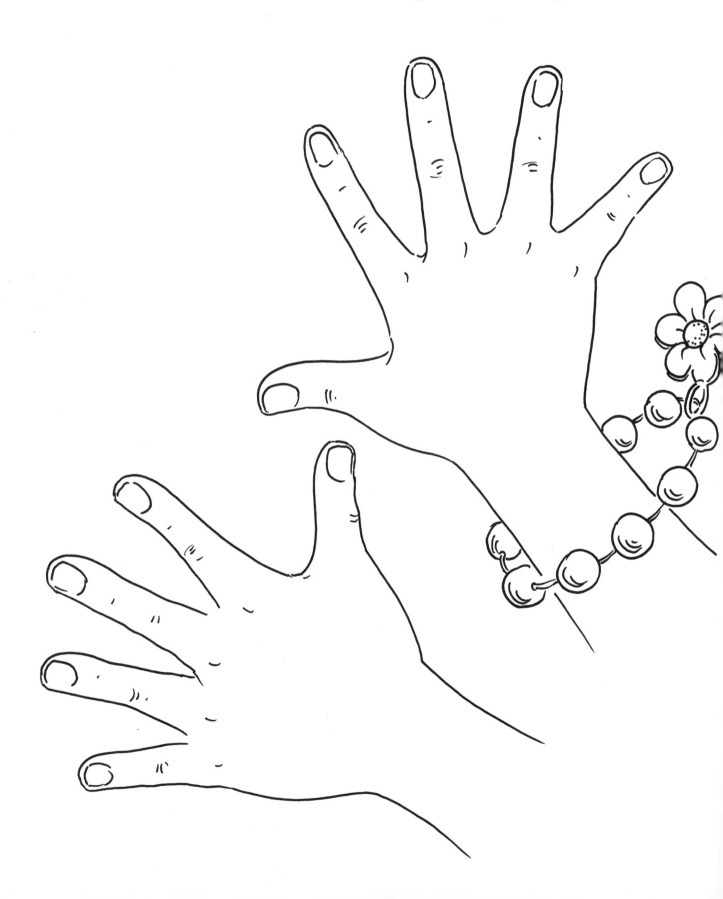

Fun in the Sun

The beach is an excellent place to go exploring.
Nancy hopes to find many treasures!
Draw her fancy fun-in-the-sun ensemble.

JoJo and Nancy see a sailboat on the ocean.
Connect the dots to see what it looks like.

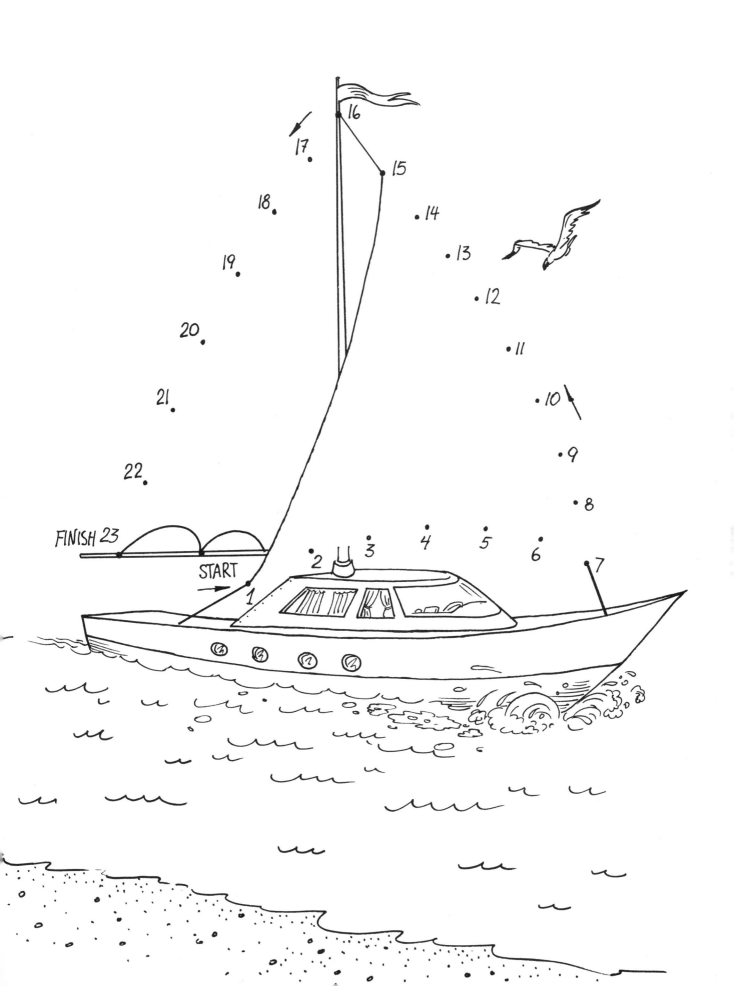

Hermit crabs are hiding in the rocks.
Can you find six of them?

The whole family builds the biggest sand castle ever.
Decorate the castle with shells, pebbles—
or anything you can think of!

It's important to stay hydrated when you're out in the sun.
(That's a fancy way of saying to drink a lot of water.)
Help Nancy and JoJo get to the snack stand, so they can
cool off with an icy cold drink.

See how many shells, starfish, and hermit crabs you can find in the scene. Circle them.

Nancy loves writing her name in the sand.
Write your name above her name.

Nancy wants to draw a picture of a crab she's found.
Draw the crab in Nancy's notebook.

Out of This World

Nancy loves exploring the sky with her telescope because
she thinks that stars are fascinating.
She especially loves seeing comets because
they are very rare. Draw the tail of this comet.

Stars that create a picture are a constellation.
Connect the dots to see what this constellation looks like.
(Hint: Its name is Ursa Major.)

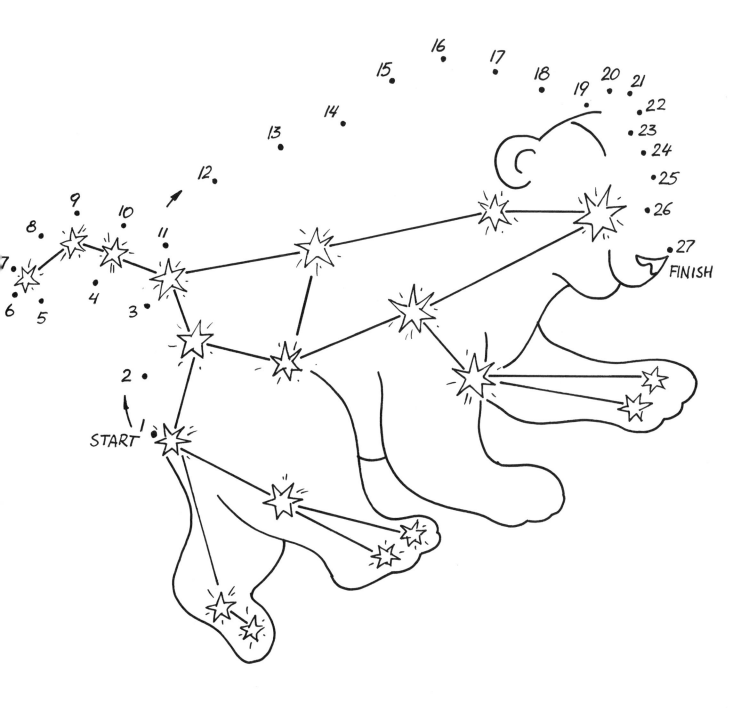

Nancy's mom bought stickers for JoJo's room.
There are stars, moons, and planets.
JoJo started putting them up, but got distracted.
Finish decorating JoJo's wall.

Nancy wants to be a fancy astronaut.
Make her space suit and helmet extra fancy!
Decorate Marabelle's space outfit too.

Nancy dreams about flying to the moon when she is older.
Help Nancy find the path from Earth to the moon!

Nancy learned all about the planets in school. Saturn is the second biggest in the solar system and has rings around it. Draw your own fancy planets in the circles.

Nancy's mom made some star-shaped cookies.
Decorate them!

Nancy's family is at the planetarium!
Nancy is looking at a model of the planet Mars.
Color the areas labeled "1" blue,
and then color the rest of Mars orange.

When US astronauts first landed on the moon, they planted an American flag. Imagine you just landed on the moon. What would your flag look like?

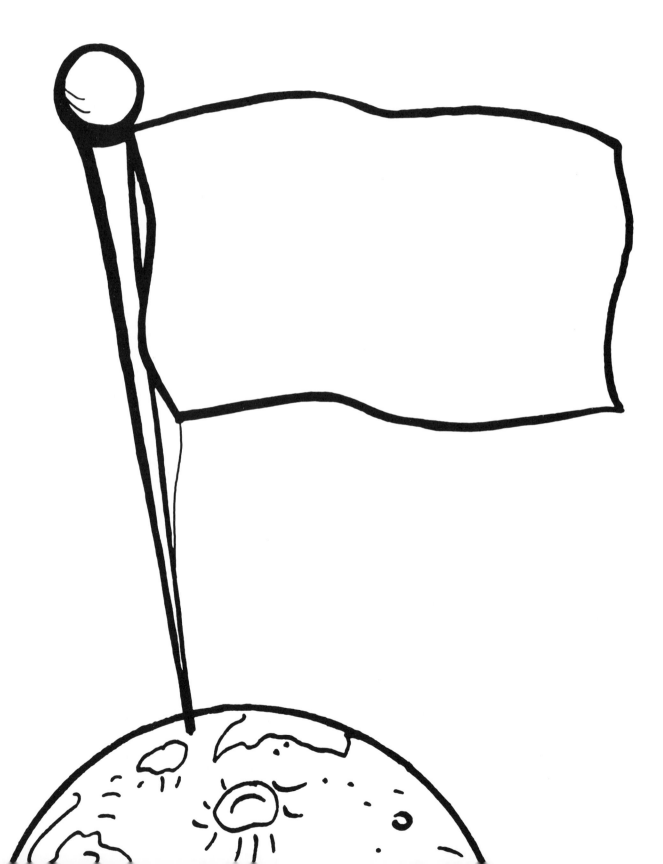

Exotic Places

Nancy loves reading about Paris and other foreign cities.
Connect the dots to draw the Eiffel Tower.

Nancy has postcards from all the places she has traveled to. Draw a line from the postcard in the album to a picture of what Nancy was wearing at that destination.

JoJo doesn't know what to pack for her trip
to visit her grandparents.
Circle the items that you think are absolutely essential
(which means she absolutely must bring them with her).

Decorate Nancy's suitcase.

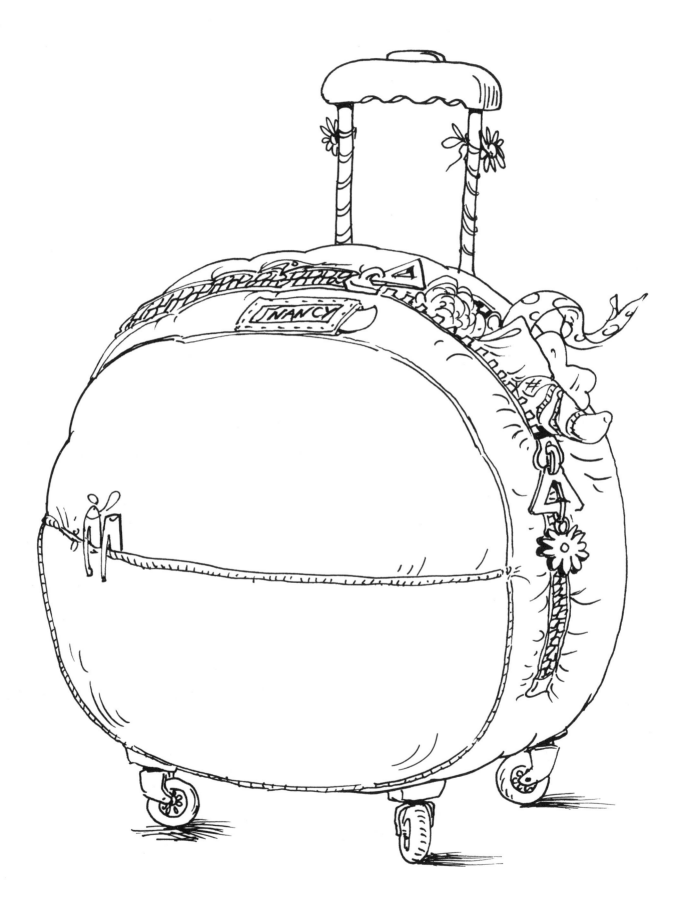

Help JoJo find her suitcase.
(Hint: It has ladybugs and dragonflies on it.)
Draw a circle around JoJo's suitcase.

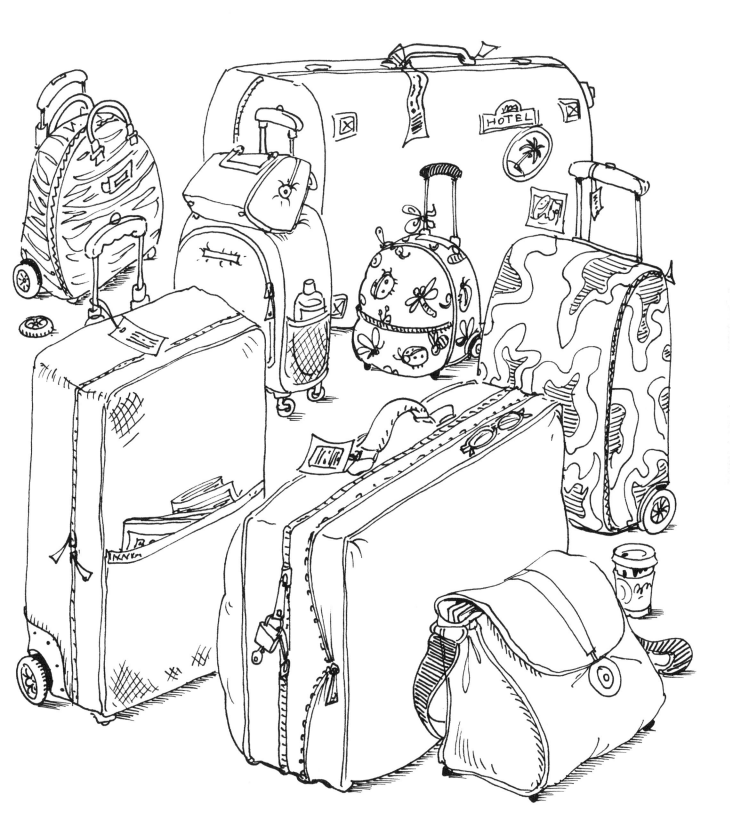

Nancy's family is taking a train to visit her grandparents.
Draw what Nancy sees out the window.

Ooh la la! The train has a snack car.
Nancy orders a delicious snack.
Draw what she is about to eat. Bon appétit!
(That's French for "enjoy your food.")

The Clancys stay at the City Squire Motel. Before dinner,
Nancy pampers herself with a luxurious bubble bath.
Draw the bubbles. Then draw bottles of shampoo,
lotion, and bath salts on the shelf.

Grandma takes Nancy and JoJo to the ballet.
Draw the tutus on the dancers.
Color in their costumes and draw the scenery.

The next day, everyone visits the art museum.
Nancy adores looking at art. It is so inspirational.
(That means it gives her ideas.)
What does this painting look like?

This painting is a still life. That means it is a painting of things that do not move, like fruit, flowers, and baskets. Color in the still life that Nancy is looking at by following the numbers that go with each color.

1: orange; 2: yellow; 3: blue; 4: pink;
5: peach; 6: lilac; 7: green

At the museum, Nancy finds an exotic mask.
(Something exotic is out of the ordinary.)
Color the mask next to it.

Nancy goes to the museum gift shop to
get Mrs. DeVine a postcard.
Draw the front of the postcard.

Nancy's family is at a botanical garden—
that's a special garden just for flowers and plants.
This bush was cut into the shape of an animal.
Connect the dots to see what it looks like.
Then draw your own animal-shaped bush.

Nancy's mom wants to take a picture
of Nancy and JoJo in the garden.
Draw the flowers around Nancy and JoJo.

Oh no! This gorgeous swan is separated from her baby.
(The fancy word for a baby swan is a cygnet.
It's pronounced SIG-nit.)
Help the mother swan get to her baby.

Look! Nancy sees a frog. Maybe he is a frog prince.
Turn him into froggy royalty
by drawing a crown and cape on him.

Here is a special garden where families can pick
their own vegetables. Poor JoJo picked a basket
of vegetables, but she dropped it.
Find the two carrots and three tomatoes she lost.
Then color in the garden.

Nancy and Bree missed each other when Nancy was away!
Help Nancy get to Bree.

Home Again!

Even though it is fun to explore someplace new,
there really is no place like home.
Now Nancy is ready for some beauty rest.
Make Nancy's bed and room as fancy as possible.

Fill this page with your fanciest doodles!

Fill this page with your fanciest doodles!

Fill this page with your fanciest doodles!